To Katie and Randy,
who missed it all.
—L. L.

To Wonmi and Hayjin, my two sisters-in-law.
Special thanks to Joshua's mother, Shilchen Lee; and Wei Zhou.
—Y. H.

Atheneum Books for Young Readers · An imprint of Simon & Schuster Children's Publishing Division · 1230 Avenue of the Americas, New York, New York 10020 · Text copyright © 2006 by Lenore Look · Illustrations copyright © 2006 by Yumi Heo · All rights reserved, including the right of reproduction in whole or in part in any form. · Book design by Polly Kanevsky and Kristin Smith · The text for this book is set in Highlander. · The illustrations for this book are rendered in oils, pencil, and collage. · Manufactured in China · First Edition · 10 9 8 7 6 5 4 3 2 1 · Library of Congress Cataloging-in-Publication Data · Look, Lenore. · Uncle Peter's amazing Chinese wedding / Lenore Look ; illustrated by Yumi Heo. · p. cm. · "An Anne Schwartz book." · Summary: A Chinese-American girl describes the festivities of her uncle's Chinese wedding and the customs behind them. · ISBN-13: 978-0-689-84458-4 · ISBN-10: 0-689-84458-1 · 1. Chinese Americans—Juvenile fiction. [1. Chinese Americans— Fiction. 2. Weddings—Fiction. 3. Nieces—Fiction.] I. Heo, Yumi, ill. II. Title. · PZ7.L8682 Un 2004 · [E]—dc21 · 2002010740

UNCLE PETER'S AMAZING CHINESE WEDDING

WRITTEN BY LENORE LOOK

ILLUSTRATED BY YUMI HEO

An Anne Schwartz Book
Atheneum Books for Young Readers
NEW YORK   LONDON   TORONTO   SYDNEY

This is Uncle Peter,
my father's baby brother,
the coolest dude, a girl's best buddy.

Today he's getting married.

Everyone is happy happy. Everyone but *me*. I love weddings, but not this one. Uncle Peter is upstairs taking his wedding bath so he'll be clean as Monday morning. Except this is Saturday, and he should be with me, getting dirty at the playground. After a hot-dog lunch, we should be heading to the movies. "Jumbo popcorn, please," he'd say. "With extra butter for my special girl."

I'm his special girl. *Just me*. I am the jelly on his toast, and the leaves in his tea. Now, I am an umbrella turned inside out. I squeeze back my tears.

Downstairs the air is thick with stories of Uncle Peter: high-school chess champion, fastest 100-meter track star, best mailman around.

Everyone is busy ooh-ing and aah-ing over the presents the bride's family gave him: a pair of shoes, so that he would go far; a wallet, to wish him wealth; a belt, to hold up his pants; a new suit, to help him look good. My aunties touch everything as though they are shopping. "*Dui ho,*" they coo, meaning "best quality."

My cousins race through Uncle Peter's house and stab one another with paper swords. Then "Start your engines!" someone yells.

It's the lucky hour for Uncle Peter to pick up his bride.
If this were a hundred years ago, she would ride in a special
chair carried by his friends. Two hundred years ago, he would
carry her on his back. But today he is using his car.

Father tells us children to go along to bring good luck.
My cousins scramble for the best seats and I end up squished.

"You can't see her yet," orders Cousin Mei-Ming, blocking Stella's door
when we get there. "Pay up."

Now the groom must bargain for the bride, to show how much
he'll give for her love.

First Uncle Peter offers bus tokens. Then an earring. Cousin Hayman
hands over his rubber-fish key chain. I give my last purple jawbreaker,
but not before scraping it just a little with my teeth. Finally Uncle Peter
gives her—yikes!—two hundred dollars.

"Not enough," says Lucy Sue, the maid of honor. "Sing us a song."

"Climb a tree!"

"Cartwheel!"

My cousins help Uncle Peter by doing everything the bridesmaids ask, until . . .

. . . here comes the bride! Amazing Stella, hair like unwoven silk, eyes like two black pearls, is dressed from head to toe in red red red to bring good luck. Dragons and phoenixes chase one another across her long, tall dress.

When Uncle Peter sees her, his face lights up like the aurora borealis and he reaches for her hand. I quick grab his other one and pull.

"Let's go," I say.

Someone pushes me here and shoves me there, until we wind up inside Stella's house, and right in place for family pictures.

There is nowhere else to stand except around Stella. She is the sun, and we are the rest of the universe.

The camera follows Stella's every move. She twinkles and shines. I feel like cosmic dust.

The camera's flash explodes, and when I blink, a lost tear slides down my cheek.

It rains birdseed and kisses when Stella and her bridesmaids, all the cousins, Uncle Peter, and I get back to his house.

"How about shooting a few hoops?" I shout to him, but he only laughs and winks at me.

Why does he think I'm joking?

Inside, the bride and groom light incense and bow to the faded photographs of Ancient-Grandpa and Ancient-Grandma. They bow to the other grown-ups, then to each other. Soon everyone is bowing, which is the Chinese way of saying, "Hello, you are important to me."

I try bowing, but Stella passes by me without a nod.

It's time for the tea ceremony where the family officially welcomes the bride. Stella will serve tea, showing she is no longer a guest but a member of the family.

Suddenly I have an idea. I sneak into the kitchen where the hot Chrysanthemum Special is waiting in Grandma's fancy pot. . . .

When Stella pours,
everyone asks, "What's this?"
and peers into their tiny cups.
It looks like water. It smells
like water. It *is* water!

"Where's the *cha*?"
Father wants to know,
and he hurries into the kitchen.

Mother looks straight at me.
"Where's the tea?" she asks.

In a quiet room I tell my mother all my sadness. Like water without tea leaves, it pours into her lap. She tells me she will be sad, too, the day I leave her. But, she says, she will also be happy, knowing I am happy. Then gently, she kisses my head.

"I will never leave," I insist.

Hungbau, red packets of lucky money, pass into Stella's and Peter's hands as they share the freshly made tea. My aunties drape Stella with buttery gold jewelry to wish her health and happiness. Father, who is funny all the time, awards Stella with a shiny medal, for "uncommon courage and bravery."

After the last drop of tea, Oldest Uncle writes Uncle Peter's Chinese name on a red cloth; then he writes Stella's. He gives them advice in Chinese, which sounds like a long, boring speech until Oldest Aunt clears her throat and gives him a little poke. The happy couple exchange rings. And then—yuck—they kiss. Everyone claps and smiles.

At last comes the fun part—the bed-jumping ceremony that ends the sleepy half of the wedding. My grandmas say that the new couple will have as many children as will jump on their bed, which is covered with a ton of sweets.

But my cousins get there before I do,
and I end up with Aunt Louise's healthy tofu chips.
"Thank you," I mumble as politely as I can.

Stella changes into her dress for the banquet. If this were a hundred years ago, she would change into a hundred different dresses to show off her family's wealth; if this were two hundred years ago, she would have to change so many times that she wouldn't be able to eat.

While Grandpa is saying that Stella's a feast for the eyes, I feast on vegetables disguised as flowers, duck with skin like paper, and my favorite—long-life noodles, too slippery for chopsticks, but perfect to slurp from the edge of my plate. The cake has extra-creamy frosting, but my favorite is the wedding soup, a sweet broth of red beans and pearl tapioca. Fertility soup, my aunties whisper, good for making babies. Gulp. "Milk, please," I cough.

There are toasts to the bride and groom—Stella, award-winning science teacher, expert car mechanic, loving daughter, and Peter, the luckiest man in town.

My cousins like clanging on their water glasses to make the bride and groom kiss, which makes me squeeze my eyes shut and Auntie Lucy cough into her napkin.

Then Stella changes into her dancing dress. Everyone
shimmies to a band called GigaDragonByte—even LoBaak,
my great-grandmother, who can still get down at 103!

I stand far back when Stella throws her bouquet, because I know she has a mean forty-yard pass. I almost catch it, but it's intercepted by Auntie Annie, who—oops!—drops it into the hands of Auntie Karen.

Before I get to dance with Uncle Peter, it's time to go. The good-bye line moves too slow for baby Henry, who's tired and cranky, but too fast for me.

Suddenly, "Come with me," someone says in my ear. It's Aunt Stella. "I nearly forgot the most important thing . . . ," she says, pulling me outside.

Stella hands me a big box. "You are my first and only niece," she says. "I want you to do this." She dashes back to the line, but not before blowing me a kiss and saying, "I hope you know I love you."

I open the box a tiny bit. A butterfly flutters out, and then another. I open it all the way, and soon the air is filled with a thousand butterflies! The sight is so beautiful I can't even breathe.

Everyone has come to join me now. They gasp and clap and I take a deep bow, and finally everything feels like it should—like a wonderful dream.

"Great job, my awesome, special girl," I hear Uncle Peter say, and he scoops me into his arms.

Aunt Stella hugs us both. "Thank you for sharing your amazing uncle," she whispers just to me. Her good-bye dress looks like summer and she smells like trees and cartwheels.

"Welcome to the family," I whisper, and hug her back before they get in their car and drive away.